FIREFIGHTERS

Paulette Bourgeois • Kim LaFave

Kids Can Press

Many thanks to the North York Fire Department
— P.B. and K.L.

Acknowledgments
Thanks to Alan R. Hayes, K. Bev Gilbert and Maureen Skinner Weiner for their review
of the revised text.

 TM Kids Can Read is a trademark of Kids Can Press Ltd.

Text © 1992 Paulette Bourgeois
Illustrations © 1992 Kim Lafave
Revised edition © 2005

Kids Can Press acknowledges the financial support of the Government of Ontario,
through the Ontario Media Development Corporation's Ontario Book Initiative;
the Ontario Arts Council; the Canada Council for the Arts; and the Government of
Canada, through the BPIDP, for our publishing activity.

Published in Canada by   Published in the U.S. by
Kids Can Press Ltd.   Kids Can Press Ltd.
29 Birch Avenue   2250 Military Road
Toronto, ON M4V 1E2   Tonawanda, NY 14150

www.kidscanpress.com

Edited by David MacDonald
Designed by Kathleen Collett
Educational consultant: Maureen Skinner Weiner, United Synagogue Day School,
Willowdale, Ontario
Canadian reviewer: K. Bev Gilbert, Office of the Fire Marshal, Ontario
U.S. reviewer: Alan R. Hayes, Germantown Fire Department, Germantown, New York
Printed and bound in China

The hardcover edition of this book is smyth sewn casebound.
The paperback edition of this book is limp sewn with a drawn-on cover.

CM 05 0 9 8 7 6 5 4 3 2 1
CM PA 05 0 9 8 7 6 5 4 3 2 1

National Library of Canada Cataloguing in Publication Data

Bourgeois, Paulette
    Firefighters / written by Paulette Bourgeois ; illustrated by Kim LaFave.

(Kids can read)
ISBN 1-55337-750-8 (bound).   ISBN 1-55337-751-6 (pbk.)

1. Fire fighters — Juvenile literature. 2. Fire extinction — Juvenile
literature. I. LaFave, Kim II. Title. III. Series: Kids Can read (Toronto, Ont.)

HD8039.F5B68 2005   j363.37'8'023   C2004-901932-5

Kids Can Press is a **ᏟᎾᏒᎢᏕ** TM Entertainment company

The firefighters are dozing. But they can
hop out of their beds and into their boots
in seconds.

A fire has started in apartment 804.

A smoke alarm beeps. Everyone leaves the building.

The superintendent calls the fire department from across the street.

The dispatcher gets the call and alerts the closest fire station.

The firefighters quickly slide down
the pole or race down the stairs. On go
the pants. On go the coats. On go the
helmets. On go the boots. Each firefighter
knows what to do.

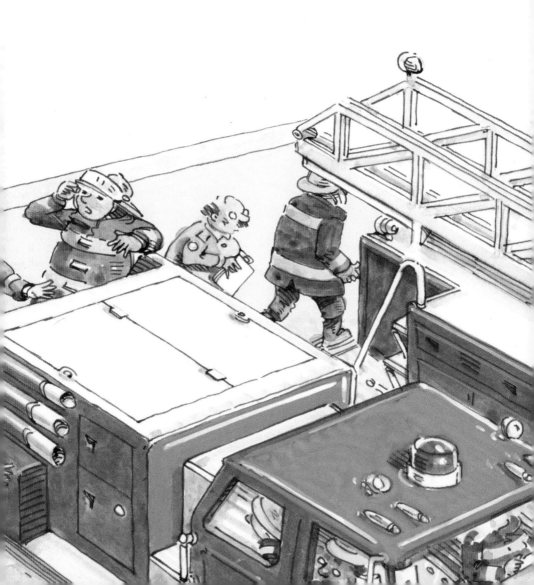

8

The firefighters climb the ladders.
They break holes in the windows so smoke
and fumes can escape. Some firefighters
check to see if anyone needs to be rescued.
Other firefighters attach hoses to hydrants.

Firefighters always bring their own air to breathe. Smoke can be just as dangerous as fire. Sometimes the smoke is so thick the firefighters can't see their own hands!

Firefighters go to the floor below the burning apartment first. There's no smoke there. They connect their hose and climb the stairs.

The firefighters smash open the door
of the apartment on fire. When they turn on
the hose, so much water gushes out that it
takes two firefighters to hold the hose.

Even when the fire is out, the job isn't done. The firefighters cut off door and window frames. They make sure nothing is burning behind the woodwork.

Then they look for the cause of the fire. "Ah, here's the answer. The plugs are frayed," says a firefighter.

Fires leave many clues about how they started.

13

Back at the station, the firefighters clean the truck and equipment. Even if they're tired, the firefighters must do this right away. The equipment has to be ready at all times.

Firefighters have their own homes and families. But the station is a second home. They sleep there on night shifts.

Sometimes it's boring at the station. Firefighters read, watch television and relax between alarms.

Firefighters must be strong enough to carry a heavy adult to safety. They need to know how fires start and how to fight any kind of fire. They also need to know how to help in an emergency.

Firefighters have to be able to free
someone trapped in a car. They have to be
able to help people who are sick or injured.

In the country, volunteers fight the fires.

A barn is burning! The farmer calls the fire number. The dispatcher alerts the volunteers. Some volunteers drive their own cars to the fire. Others go to the fire station and get the fire truck.

There are no fire hydrants in the country. The firefighters bring their own water. They can also pump water from ponds, rivers and lakes.

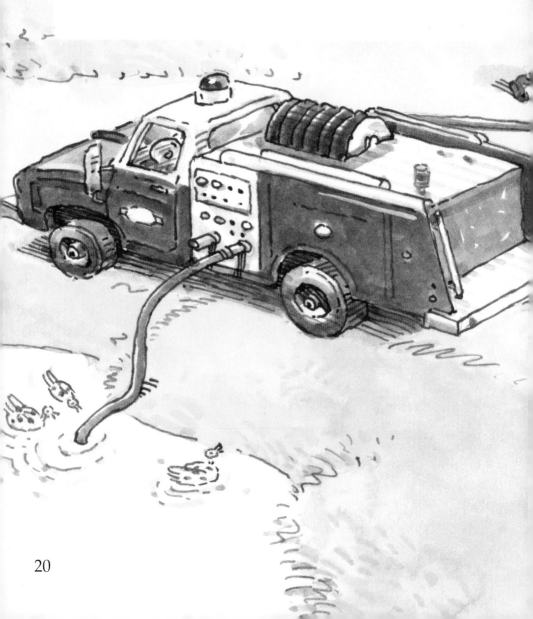

Water bombers dump water on forest fires.

The firefighters dig trenches to stop the fire from spreading. They also try to smother flames with water or dirt. Sometimes there are no roads close to a forest fire. Firefighters have to walk from the nearest road.

How to Prevent Fires

1. Make sure you have a working smoke alarm on every floor and outside every sleeping area.

2. Make sure cords are not frayed. Never put cords under rugs or carpets.

3. Keep a working fire extinguisher outside the kitchen and in the car. Everyone should know how to use it.

4. Make sure there is only one plug in each receptacle.

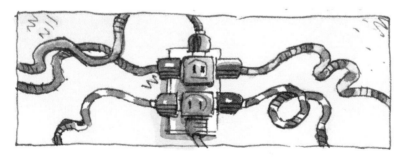

5. Never leave a candle burning if no one is in the room. Make sure pets can't get close to burning candles.

6. Anything with this sign on it should be kept away from open flame and used with care.

7. Never touch matches or lighters.

8. Make sure an adult is always in the kitchen when food is being cooked.

How to Keep Safe

1. Make a family escape plan for your home. Plan two ways to get out of each room. For some rooms, you may need to buy a hanging ladder to escape out a window.

2. Decide on a safe place for the family to meet if you must leave your house. Once you get out of a burning building, you must always stay out!

3. Have home fire drills.

4. Learn the number for the fire department. If you have to call, give your name, address and the nearest intersection. Never call from inside a burning building. Get out and look for somewhere else you can call from.

How to Stay Safe in a Fire

If there's smoke or fire, yell "Fire!"

If there is smoke, hold a cloth or towel (wet is best) over your mouth and nose. Crawl on the floor to your escape route.

Feel doors before opening them. If a door is hot, don't open it. Put a blanket or towel (wet is best) at the bottom of the door to stop smoke from coming in.

If your escape window won't open, throw a chair or other heavy object into the glass to break it. Clear away broken glass before climbing out. Phone the fire department from another building.

Never, never hide — get out!

Never look for pets or toys — get out!

Firefighters may look and sound strange, but they are there to help. Do not run away from them.

If your clothes catch fire, never run! Stop! Drop to the ground. Roll until the flames are out.

How to Stay Safe in an Apartment Fire

Close all windows, then make sure everyone leaves the apartment. Carry your key in case smoke or fire forces you to go back inside.

Close the door. Go to a fire exit quickly and calmly.

If your door is hot or smoke is coming through, stay in your apartment. If you see smoke in the hallway, go back to your apartment. Shut the door and put wet blankets or towels at the base of the door.

Open a window and yell "Fire!" Call the fire department and let them know where you are.

Never use the elevators during a fire. Use the fire exit and leave the building.

If one escape stairwell is smoky, use the other staircase. If that one is smoky too, go back to your apartment.

If the fire is in your apartment, yell "Fire!" Get everyone out. Pull the alarm in the hallway. It may not be connected to the fire department. Once you get to a safe place, call the fire emergency number.

Remember, if you act fire smart, you'll stay fire safe.